The Boy who sailed with Columbus

The Boy who sailed with Columbus

Text by MICHAEL FOREMAN
and RICHARD SEAVER

Illustrations by MICHAEL FOREMAN

Arcade Publishing · New York
Little, Brown and Company

First U.S. Edition 1992

ISBN 1-55970-178-1
Library of Congress Catalog Card Number 91-55518
Library of Congress Cataloging-in-Publication information
is available.

Published in the United States by Arcade Publishing, Inc.,
New York, a Little, Brown company

10 9 8 7 6 5 4 3 2 1

Designed by Janet James

PRINTED IN ITALY

The Monastery

The monastery of La Rabida sat on a high bluff overlooking the Rio Tinto and the port of Palos in western Spain. It was an ideal place from which to watch the comings and goings of the ships, from small fishing boats to grand galleons.

Leif loved to watch the ships, because it made him feel closer to his father, who one day five years before had sailed with the tide, never to return. Leif could hardly remember his mother, who had died when he was very young. But in his dreams he still clearly saw his father, tall with blond hair just like his own, and with the bluest eyes in all Spain. He also remembered the stories his father used to tell, of his homeland far away in the cold north, a land of snow and ice, a land of Vikings. Leif had been named after the most famous Viking of all, who, it was said, had crossed the great western ocean centuries ago and found a new land.

Since his father's disappearance, Leif had been looked after by the good monks of La Rabida, and in return for his board and keep, and his lessons, he worked in the gardens. Sometimes the sailors from Palos would climb the steep path to the monastery, to give thanks for their safe return after a voyage at sea. Leif knew that the sailors thought of the ocean as a place of storms and monsters, a place where, if you reached the edge, your ship could fall off into the great void. But despite its dangers, the ocean was where his father had gone. And now that he was twelve, it was where Leif longed to go, too.

The Navigator and His Son

Leif saw the man and boy arrive at the monastery, tired and dusty from their journey. They disappeared inside, but before long the boy, whose name was Diego, was back out into the sunshine, exploring the surroundings. Leif was two years older than Diego, but over the next few weeks they became firm friends.

While his father talked endlessly with the Prior, Diego helped Leif in the garden. And in the evenings, before the final prayers and singing of the psalms, the two boys would sit among the pine trees overlooking the harbor and talk of the ocean and of their fathers' many adventures. Diego's father was a navigator from Italy who had survived many dangerous adventures, and even a shipwreck. Now his father was planning a great venture. He had already gone seeking money in the cities of England, Holland, and France, and Diego was full of stories about the palaces and cathedrals there, and of the crowded dirty streets all around.

"What kind of great adventure?" Leif wanted to know.

"To cross the western ocean," Diego said.

"But isn't he afraid of falling off the edge if he goes too far?"

"My father says the world isn't flat," Diego said, feeling proud to know more than his older friend. "It's round, just like this stone. So by sailing west, he'll reach Japan, China, and India, with all their riches." He turned the stone in his hand, to show the route his father would take.

Leif had heard of those far-off places, but in his lessons he had learned you had to travel *east* to reach them. But still, if the earth really *was* round . . .

"The Prior of La Rabida believes my father," Diego was saying. "In fact, he has written to the King and Queen asking for their help."

Several days later Diego ran into the garden, shouting the news. "They've said yes!" he said. "They've given father the money! The ships are being outfitted down below in Palos. And father's already recruiting men to sail with him."

Leif knew that such ships usually had one or two boys in each crew. Diego was too young. But he, Leif, should be just old enough . . .

"Please talk to your father about me, Diego. Tell him my father was a Viking. And a great sailor."

In fact, the monks had already told Diego's father about Leif, about his fine character, his Viking blood, and his strong, clear singing voice.

That evening Diego's father came to the two boys in the pines. He laid a hand on Leif's shoulder and said: "Leif, Diego has spoken to me about you, as have the Holy Fathers. I hear you want to sail with me. Well, sail you shall, as ship's boy on my flagship, the *Santa Maria*."

However much he had dared hope, Leif found it hard to believe. To sail on the great seas, just as his father had!

"And I hear you have a fine singing voice," said Diego's father. "On board, you shall sing the Angelus every evening."

Leif looked down in the misty sunset at the cluster of ships being prepared. Was it true? When they sailed, he would be on the flagship! He looked up at the man above him. He would never again think of him as Diego's father. From now on he was Captain-General Christopher Columbus.

The *Nina*, the *Pinta*, and the *Santa Maria*

On Friday, August 3rd, 1492, the three ships – the *Santa Maria*, the *Nina*, and the *Pinta* – sailed on the dawn tide past the monastery toward the open sea. In the lead was the *Santa Maria*, captained by Columbus. The two smaller ships were owned by one of the leading families of Palos, the Pinzons, and three members of the Pinzon family were aboard: Vincent Pinzon as captain of the *Nina*, and Martin Alonso as captain of the *Pinta*, with his brother Francisco Martin Pinzon as master of the same ship.

There was a crew of twenty on each of the smaller ships and thirty on the *Santa Maria*, as well as a surgeon, a master gunner, and some royal officials who planned to look after the gold and other treasure they expected to bring home. There was also a Master of Languages on board who could speak most European languages and Latin, Hebrew, Aramaic, and Arabic.

The captains and royal officials were housed below, but everyone else had to sleep on deck on makeshift straw mattresses. The food – which was cooked on deck – consisted of dried peas and beans, salted meat, sardines in brine, honey, and dried grapes. In place of bread – which quickly went moldy at sea – they had hardtack, which were dry biscuits. And, to drink, both wine and water.

Leif could feel his heart pounding as the ship moved out into the ocean. Did it really end, somewhere far out there? The thought filled him with a sudden fear, but then he remembered his father and felt better. Besides, he knew that several days beyond the horizon lay the Canary Islands – the Isles of Dogs – where they would stop to take on more supplies, so the ocean *couldn't* end before then.

Four days out, there was a great hue and cry aboard the *Pinta*, which seemed suddenly to lose both speed and direction at once, and began to move strangely like some wounded beast. Both the *Nina* and *Santa Maria* changed course to help their sister ship. "It's the rudder," shouted Francisco Martin Pinzon when the other ships were within hailing distance. "It's broken free!"

Fortunately the ships all carried rope, tools, and extra timber, and before long they had lashed the rudder into place, enough so the ship could maneuver. Six days later the little fleet reached the mountainous island of Tenerife without further incident. There they set about making proper repairs to the *Pinta*, which took longer than they had expected. Leif watched Columbus as the Captain supervised the work, his normally impassive face growing more and more concerned with each passing day. He would glance heavenward, scowling as clouds gathered above, and Leif heard him more than once mutter to himself about "the precious time we are losing."

One evening, during the Angelus, just as Leif was reaching for the closing notes of his hymn, there was a rumbling, faint at first then louder and louder, till all at once the mountain above seemed to explode. Some of the crew dropped to their knees in fear, and Leif almost did too, but he was standing next to Columbus, who was gazing at the spectacle in quiet awe, and he did not want to seem a coward.

"It's nothing to fear," Columbus said softly, "but one of Nature's splendors. Her way of venting the pressures that build within earth's depths. I have seen it before, at Mount Etna in Sicily years ago. A volcano, named after the Roman god of fire, Vulcan. Instead of losing your heads, get up and enjoy the incredible beauty of it!"

The men sheepishly got to their feet, and all watched in silence as the mountain spewed fire and lava from its glowing peak. Leif was silently proud he had remained standing, and once, glancing over at Columbus, he thought he saw a slight nod of approval from the Captain.

On the morning of September 6th, all three ships were buzzing with activity as the crews brought the last supplies of food and water on board. Just before noon they left the harbor. Leif watched the buildings on shore grow smaller and smaller, and he wondered, with a twinge of fear, if he would ever see them again. He glanced over at the Captain, whose strong face and erect bearing again filled him with courage.

There was little wind, however, and for most of that day and the next the sails flopped aimlessly and the ships barely moved. But finally, on Saturday the 8th, they caught a good northeast breeze and began to move smartly southwest. By the next day, all sight of land had disappeared. Ahead of them lay the vast, surging ocean and the great adventure.

The Great Adventure

To keep time on board, a half-hour sandglass was kept next to the compass on the poop deck. It was Leif's job to turn it as soon as the last grains of sand had run through. It was a trying job, for he had to be careful not to nod off or daydream. But at night especially, when it often grew cool and the hours dragged, Leif was tempted to wrap his hands around the glass to warm it and make the sand run through faster.

That must have been an old trick on the part of duty boys, however, for on the first day out they were warned by the helmsman that if ever they should yield to such temptations they would be severely punished.

"Navigation is very delicate, and should the time of the sandglass be changed, it could lead to all kinds of serious errors. Do you understand?"

The duty boys nodded. "Yes, sir," they said as one. "We do, sir."

They had food and water for thirty days, for no one – not even the Captain-General, Leif suspected – knew how long their trip would take. But from the third day out men were posted on lookout duty, one at the bow of each ship, one aloft in the crow's nest on the mainmast.

"Look out not only for land, men," the first mate said, "but for any telltale signs that land might be close: drifting twigs, weeds, changes in sea color, unusual cloud shapes, birds."

On the tenth day a shout rang out: "Weeds! Heavy drifts of it ahead!"

The crew rushed to the bow. There was so much seaweed it almost obscured the sea itself, so that it looked as though they were sailing through a gently rolling field.

"It must mean the water's shallow here," one sailor said, knowingly.

"And doesn't shallow water mean land is near?" added another, hopefully.

But for three days they sailed on through the weeds, with no sighting of land. Leif was fascinated by the waving fronds and, during his watch, peered at them intently, making up stories about the sea people who lived down below in those watery fields. All of a sudden he saw something clinging to the fronds. "A crab," he shouted, "a live crab!" And didn't crabs live near shore?

They fished it out and brought it to Columbus, who inspected it carefully. If he had any thoughts about it, he did not share them. Then another shout, this time from the crow's nest:
"Birds, sir! Two birds off the port bow!"

They were identified as booby birds, and at their sighting the men's spirits rose. But soon the birds disappeared, and no others were sighted. Finally the weed thinned, then vanished, and they broke into clear water. But the crews greeted the change not with relief but with growing concern, for by now they were fourteen days out, and half the provisions were gone. To make matters worse, the winds were light and progress slow. Leif heard the men talking among themselves.

Booby birds

Tern

"I helped load this ship," one said, "and if the Captain doesn't turn back soon, we'll not have enough food and water to carry us back to the Canaries."

But Columbus's spirits seemed as high as ever. "Look," he would say, as a falling star streaked across the night sky. "Is that not a sign from God?" Or, when it rained, he would say: "You see, another sign that God is watching over us and adding to our supply of fresh water."

Then more booby birds were sighted, and a single tern. The men's spirits, which seemed to Leif to rise and fall as swiftly and endlessly as the rolling waves, again soared.

Later next evening, while Leif was on deck, he saw a huge creature on the horizon, looking like a moving hulk of land. "Whale off the port beam!" came the shout from the crow's nest. Leif saw a graceful arc of water – not unlike the fountain on the town square back in Palos – rise and fall, then the whale dived and disappeared with a great thwack of its tail. Leif shook his head in wonder at the size, strength, and beauty of the beast.

Several days went by, and each day Leif could feel the men's spirits drop little by little, and their mutterings grow, especially after the rations were cut. It worried him, so that he had trouble sleeping at night, but he kept telling himself to have faith in the Captain, and finally he would nod off.

On the evening of their twentieth day out – September 25th – a shout came from the captain of the *Pinta*. "*Tierra! Tierra!* Land ho!" Crews from all three ships swarmed up the rigging and peered into the distance, calling to each other, "Yes! There it is!" Columbus himself could see it and Leif saw him drop to his knees and call the crew to a prayer of thanksgiving. Leif joined in the prayers but continued to stare at the horizon. To his young clear eyes it looked like nothing more than a cloud.

As dawn broke, the crews realized that the "land" had in fact been only a thick cloud mass. Leif saw the men gather in small groups and knew what they were saying. Whenever he approached, they suddenly fell silent, for they knew he had been personally chosen by the Captain and might take their remarks back to him. But once, when he was in the shadow of a gunwale, he heard one of the men, whom he could not identify by voice, say something that chilled his heart:

"I say let's throw him overboard and sail for home!"

"I agree. The man's mad. Totally mad."

"You forget," said a voice Leif did recognize, that of the third mate. "We're twenty-one days out. We've rations for maybe another ten days. Two weeks at best. We *can't* turn back."

frigate bird

And so they sailed into October, fearful of what lay ahead but knowing they had no choice. Playful dolphins followed in their wake, which again Columbus took as a good sign. "It won't be long now," he reassured them. "And that being so, let's give a prize to the man and ship to sight land first." That simple challenge seemed to stir the crew's spirits and focus their minds. Since the *Pinta* and *Nina* were faster than the larger *Santa Maria*, they had an advantage and sailed far ahead, sometimes out of sight, so that Columbus was forced to issue an order: every day at dawn and sunset the ships should come together. There may have been another reason for the order: at dawn and sunset there was less sea haze and visibility was best. Thus if land were sighted, it would most likely be then. And since the *Santa Maria*'s crow's nest was higher than those of her sister ships, chances were Columbus's own ship would win the prize!

Rations were nearly exhausted, but sometimes frigate birds and other tropical birds alighted on the ships and were snared by the crew. And occasionally flying fish would flop onto the deck, as though sent by heaven, to augment the rations and revive the men's flagging courage.

At sunrise on Sunday, October 7th, the *Pinta*, which was some distance ahead of the other two ships, fired one of her guns – the signal that land had been sighted. Again the men swarmed up the rigging, laughing and shouting, but soon grew still: it was another false alarm.

That night, throughout his watch, Leif heard birds flying overhead in great numbers. Next morning the sky was still speckled with birds. Columbus, perhaps in desperation, or reading it as another sign from heaven, changed course slightly and followed the birds.

There was a good breeze, too. The ships moved briskly ahead, and the crews of all three ships, as though now believing land might really be near, scanned the horizon expectantly. Hour by hour there were little encouraging signs: fresh green seaweed; a small stick; and, from the *Nina*, a twig with a flower.

At ten o'clock at night on October 11th – their thirty-sixth day at sea – Columbus, who was standing on the sterncastle, gave a shout: "Light ahead!"

There was silence as everyone peered into the darkness. Nothing. But then Leif's young eyes saw it again. "There it is!" he shouted. And this time all saw it, and a great shout went up from the three ships. The men's eyes followed the flickering light, which came and went as though it were a lantern on a boat that rose and fell with the waves, or perhaps a light being carried among the trees. But this time there was no doubt: it *was* a light.

Four hours later land was sighted. Cliffs pale in the moonlight, darker patches of trees. Not a trick of light or cloud this time but *tierra* – real, solid land.

All but the mainsails were furled. And the crew, exhausted and elated, waited for dawn to break.

Landfall

At first light sails were unfurled and all flags hoisted. Now they had to find a safe channel through the reef which lay between them and the sweet-smelling land.

Once through the reef Columbus put on his best scarlet doublet and, with officers in their finest uniforms and some archers, set off in the small boat to stake his claim to the New World.

They waded through the shallows, Columbus holding the Royal standard aloft, Leif trying to keep its tasseled ends from trailing in the surf.

Columbus named the island San Salvador, the island of the Holy Savior, claimed it for the King and Queen of Spain, and said a prayer which was chorused by all on the beach and echoed across the water by those still on the ships.

There was movement among the trees. Slight at first. Moving shadows. Fingers tightened on swords and crossbows. Leif was glad to be partly hidden by the Royal banner. A group of people cautiously emerged from the trees. There were men and women, dark-haired and naked. Some were heavily painted in red, white, and black. They were unarmed except for wooden spears, some edged with fish teeth.

While they could not understand each other, and the Master of Languages proved no help, Columbus used sign language to ask what their land was called. "Guanahani," they said, repeating it several times.

The people of Guanahani seemed gentle, but Leif was both fascinated and afraid of their looks, for many had terrible scars on their bodies, as though from battle. Still in sign language they explained that they were sometimes attacked by warlike people from a nearby land.

"This 'nearby land,'" Columbus explained to the royal officials and Master of Languages (and to Leif, who was standing next to him), "can only be Japan. Which means we have made landfall in the ocean of the Indies."

They stayed at Guanahani for two days, replenishing their water and food supply from the island. They gave the "Indians," as Columbus now called them, gifts of beads and little brass bells, which seemed to delight them. In return, the natives gave them spears and balls of cotton. "It's not gold," one of the officials said, referring to the cotton, "but it's still a valuable crop."

Leif heard Columbus and the other leaders of the fleet talking among themselves, and he thought he heard them say something about "capturing the Indians." He hoped not: they seemed so kind and gentle. Why would anyone want to capture them? But late that afternoon – Sunday – he saw the rowboats that had been sent out earlier to circle the island returning with seven "Indians" on board.

Leif didn't dare ask, but he was glad when he heard one of the royal officials ask the captain what he planned to do with them.

"Take them back to Spain," he said, "as living specimens. Proof that we reached our goal. Besides, we can try to teach them Spanish, so that they can interpret for us on future voyages."

The royal officials nodded wisely; clearly the idea made good sense to them.

That evening the fleet set sail, and Columbus was confident that Japan would soon be reached. He soon saw so many islands dotted along the horizon he was unsure which to explore first.

They steered toward what appeared to be the largest. As they neared land, several canoes put out to sea and paddled in their direction. When they were near, two of the captives on the *Santa Maria* made a dash for the side of the ship, and, before anyone could stop them, jumped overboard and were hauled up into the canoes. One islander, however, paddled his canoe close to the *Santa Maria*, hoping to trade a ball of cotton for a brass trinket, and was captured and taken to Columbus. The Captain smiled and gave the man a Spanish cap, some beads, and two small bells to wear in his ears. Then he ordered the crew to help him back into his canoe. He paddled quickly to shore, where Leif saw that he was surrounded by a crowd of villagers – the sound of their excited voices reached all the way out to the ship – to examine his trinkets.

Later three boats put ashore, with Leif aboard one, to visit the new "Indians," who again were friendly.

The cotton balls the islanders had traded did not come from planted fields, they learned, but from wild cotton. But beans, corn, and root vegetables were cultivated in small fields.

Several villagers came over to Leif and gazed in wonder at the color of his hair. Some even touched it, shyly, as though it were magic. Leif noted that many villagers wore small pieces of gold jewelry, and wondered if Columbus would notice it too, for he knew that was what they were really seeking. Not only did he notice, he asked the "Indians" where it came from, and their gestures seemed to say "from not far away."

Throughout the rest of October and November the fleet sailed from island to island. Navigating around so many uncharted islands was not as dangerous as Columbus and his fellow captains had feared. The sea was so clear that the dark areas of rock were easily spotted. Offshore it was deep blue, where Leif loved to watch the dolphins play. And in the shallow water he spent hours gazing down at the shoals of fish, of countless shapes and colors, dashing to and fro. He knew the sailors had set sail fearing sea monsters and hoping for gold. But to Leif's young eyes the ocean was revealing to him jewels far more beautiful than gold.

And the land was beautiful, too. The flowered plants and vines were of every possible color, and the trees strange and different from any he had ever seen. To himself he called them the "perfumed islands" because of the rich fragrance of the flowers. Even more colorful than the flowers were the brightly hued birds, whose high-pitched songs stilled only at night.

Though it was now November, Leif marveled at the comforting warmth of the climate – far warmer than back home. Once with the captain he visited a village, which consisted of a dozen small huts made of stout branches and covered with straw and palm leaves. Inside, the floor was of dirt, but swept clean. Instead of beds the people slept on a sling suspended between two posts, which they called *hamaca* – a hammock.

It was nearing the end of November, and the Pinzons wanted to press on in search of the place where gold might be found. But Columbus felt he had to go ashore and claim each island for King Ferdinand and Queen Isabella. On November 21st, as dawn broke and Leif prepared to wake the morning watch, he looked astern and saw that only the *Nina* was there. Sometime during the night the captain and crew of the *Pinta* had slipped anchor and set off on their own.

Columbus was furious. He paced the deck, his face red with anger, unable to contain himself. It was the only time that Leif had seen the Captain this way, and it upset him. It upset him even more when, the very next day, as they set sail, he saw that a dozen men, women, and children who had been invited on board were being detained.

Suddenly, from the sea below, Leif heard a heartrending shout. He looked and saw one of the natives standing in a canoe, his hands raised toward them. Leif would never forget the look of grief on his face.

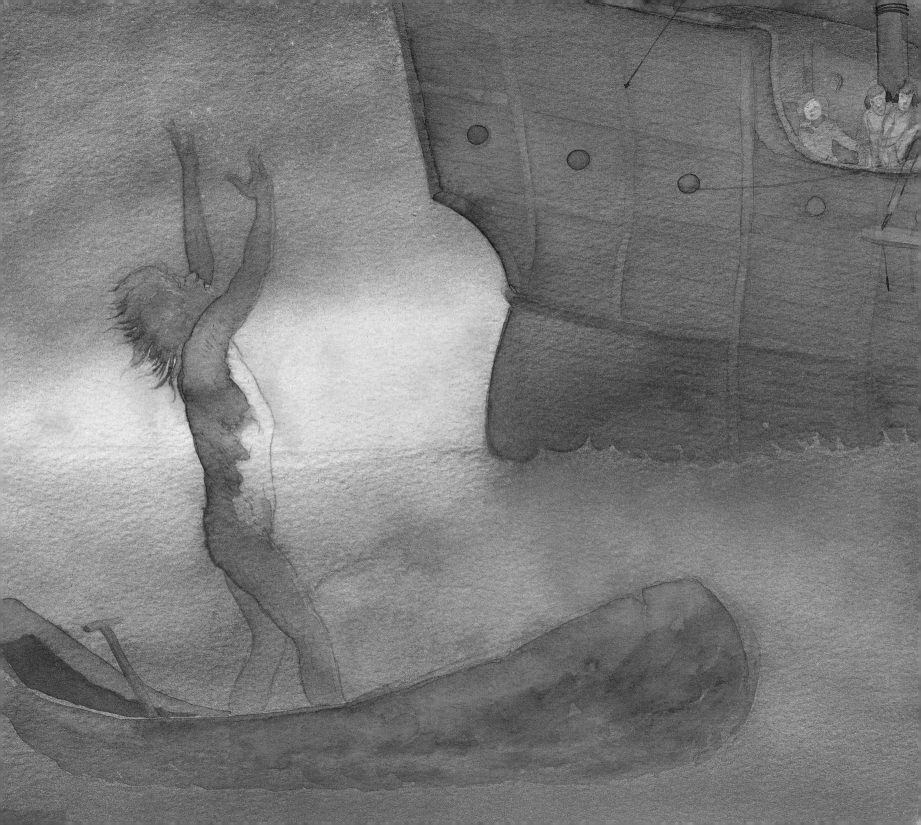

He was the father of some of the children in the
group. He begged to be allowed to join his
family in captivity. Columbus had the man pulled
on board and added to the captives, pleased to
have a "volunteer" living specimen. But Leif felt
sick and ashamed. What right did they have to take
these people from their magic island? Somehow the
great adventure did not seem so glorious after all.

It was coming up to Christmas, and for a moment Leif had a pang of homesickness
for La Rabida and the holy season there. It was so warm here that Leif had trouble even
imagining it was the time of the nativity.

On December 20th, just before nightfall, the *Santa Maria* and the *Nina* arrived in a
great natural harbor, which Columbus promptly named Puerto de la Mer Santo Tomas.

Leif saw a flood of islanders running toward the sea. They bore gifts of food, gourds
filled with fresh water, brilliantly colored parrots, and trinkets of gold. Again Columbus
and his men traded worthless glass beads for gold while Leif and the other ship's boys
traded bits of broken crockery for the islanders' spears.

Columbus pointed to the gold trinkets and said: "These. Where do these come from?"

The islanders understood and pointed toward the west.

"Is it far?" Columbus asked.

No, they seemed to say, not far at all.

They stayed for three more days on the island, feasting late into the night, but finally set sail on Christmas Eve. They sailed late, to catch the offshore winds, but as soon as they passed the reef the winds died down. Columbus had not slept for two days and a night, but still he took the first watch. At eleven o'clock he turned the wheel over to the helmsman and retired below.

Before long the helmsman, who had feasted long and hard, grew heavy-lidded and, seeing Leif beside the sandglass, gazing wistfully back toward land, said: "Take the tiller for a while, hold it firm, and make sure to keep the star just to the left of the mainmast."

The two ships drifted in the sleepy, windless swells, their crews lost in dreams of gold and Christmas.

Leif was tired too, and did his best to keep the star to the left of the mainmast. Just for a moment he decided to lay his head on the arm that held the tiller. Just for a moment . . . suddenly he felt the ship shudder beneath him and he jumped awake. But it was too late; the keel had hit the reef, and Leif could hear the timbers grind and shake.

Columbus was the first on deck. "Man the small boat!" he ordered. "If we pull hard enough, we may tow her free. Quick now! We've no time to lose!"

The men lowered the small boat, but instead of obeying orders, they rowed furiously toward the *Nina*, their fear of drowning overcoming their dread of the Captain's anger.

"Bring down the mainmast," Columbus ordered. "We've got to lighten ship!"

From the shadows to which he had retreated in shame – for he knew the fault was his – Leif watched as they cut down the mainmast. But by now the ship was swinging broadside into the reef and the sharp coral was biting into its ribs. Leif could hear the timbers breaking and knew the ship was lost. Would he drown? He knew how to swim, but when the waters came rushing in . . .

The islanders saw what had happened and put out in a fleet of canoes. They arrived just as the timbers of the *Santa Maria* finally broke and the sea flooded the hold. They managed to save not only the crew but much of the stores as well.

Several days later Columbus called upon the chief of the islanders and said, using sign language to help: "We thank you for coming to our rescue, for saving our souls and stores. You tell us you have enemies from the islands around. Well, I will leave some of my men with you to help fight off any attack."

Leif wondered if the Captain's method of thanking the islanders was not also his way of solving a serious problem he faced: with only one ship remaining, he would *have* to leave more than half the men behind.

Columbus picked thirty-five men and three officers to stay on the island, and included carpenters and caulkers who could build a fort from the timbers of the wrecked *Santa Maria*. "With your guns and the cannon from the ship you will be safe. Learn the language and gather as much information as you can until I return. You will all be well rewarded," Columbus said, and then he turned to Leif. "As punishment for falling asleep, lad, you too will remain behind."

Punishment? Leif felt a tiny knot of fear, but secretly he was excited to be left behind. He was intrigued by the people and the scents and life of the islands. Maybe *this* was the great adventure.

On Friday, January 4th, Columbus and twenty-five men set sail from the bay he had aptly named Puerto de la Navidad, Christmas Harbor. Watching the *Nina*'s sails grow smaller and smaller, Leif wondered if he would ever see Columbus again.

Fearing a possible attack, the men set about building the fort. When that work was done they had little to keep them busy. The officers began quarreling among themselves, and the sailors began wandering farther and farther from the fort, in search of gold.

Leif spent most of his time with the local boys, fishing and gathering fruit. At night he climbed into his hammock, set up among theirs, and slowly learned their language. During the day he would try to tell them about the other world across the water. He drew pictures in the sand of soldiers on horseback, of carriages and clothing, of palaces and cathedrals, and of the sea monsters they had feared but never met. But the picture they liked most, that always made them laugh, was the one he drew of a cow.

The Attack

The attack came in the middle of the night. There were only ten men in the fort, and no sentries had been posted. Within minutes all four walls were ablaze. Some villagers ran to help the Europeans, but it was too late.

Then the attackers turned on the village itself. Leif's first instinct had been to help the sailors, but he saw that was useless. He and the other boys started to run, but where? The light from the burning fort was eerie, and the night was filled with smoke and screams. Leif's heart was pounding as he covered his head and tried to run. Then he felt a blinding pain, and all turned black.

When he came to, Leif felt again the rolling swell of the sea and heard the rapid slap of water close to his ear. He knew he was in a canoe. Painfully he opened one eye and felt blood caked on his eyelids. His head throbbed in time to the grunts of the men and the splash of paddles. At least he was alive . . . then everything went black again.

When next he awoke it was to the pale light of dawn. Now he could feel other bodies stirring beside him, and though he could not see them, he suspected they were probably his friends. Finally the canoes were run up on a beach, and the boys were dragged out and tied together at the ankle and neck. A large crowd surrounded them, pushing and shouting, and several came up to Leif and tugged at his hair till it hurt.

Leif wished that he had never fallen asleep at the tiller, that he was safely back on the *Nina*, or at La Rabida. Now maybe he would be a slave, for he had heard stories of how some island tribes attacked others only to capture slaves. Or maybe these people were the feared Caribs the friendly islanders had warned Columbus about. The Caribs, they had said, were cannibals, and all of a sudden Leif pictured himself and his friends being prepared for a great feast.

A man approached, pointed to Leif, and muttered something he could not understand. He was separated from his friends, bound hand and foot, and shoved into an even larger canoe, which was pushed out through the surf as ten men clambered on board. Looking back as the canoe crested a wave, Leif could see his friends being led by the islanders into the trees. From the crest of the next wave he saw only trees. He never saw his friends again.

The men took turns paddling and made good speed through the water. Every now and then one of them held a gourd of water to Leif's lips. If they meant to kill him, why would they be caring for him? The sun set and still they paddled on. Leif dozed and dreamed of Spain, of Columbus, of his native friends, of the fort at Navidad all in flames. He awoke from time to time, then drifted back to sleep as the stars wheeled through the night sky.

Leif thought that by now Columbus should have arrived back in Spain. He might even be returning with a new, larger fleet to reinforce the settlement at Navidad and search for the great land in the west. Leif thought that perhaps one day he would be rescued and would return to Spain.

He awoke finally to see the canoe entering the mouth of a broad river. The morning mist was rising, and Leif could see canoes drawn up on both banks. Children ran through the shallows, keeping pace with the canoe, until finally it turned to shore. He was lifted from the canoe and his bonds were cut. He rubbed his wrists and ankles together, feeling exposed and awkward. There was great excitement at the sight of fair-haired Leif.

At last the crowd parted, and two old men approached.

The smaller man wore a cloak of feathers and several rows of gold, shell, and feather necklaces. The other man was tall and dressed in a manner unlike any islander Leif had yet seen. His clothing was of buckskin, his cloak of shaggy hide covered in designs. His long white hair was bound with strips of leather decorated with tiny shells.

He walked straight up to Leif and grabbed him by the shoulders, then his hands moved swiftly to Leif's throat. His face was like a mask, his eyes expressionless. Then he smiled with his mouth, but not his eyes. His eyes were dead. Two opaque globes. Like moons. His fingers touched Leif's hair.

Then he said something to the other old man, who smiled and shouted his reply, and the whole crowd echoed the cry and continued shouting as Leif was led into the village.

The village was on a rise of ground beyond the fringe of trees. Leif saw small cultivated fields. Inside one of the smaller houses he was given water and food. The wound on his head and the cuts and grazes he had received during the past two hectic days were treated with oils and ointments, and soon he fell into a deep sleep.

He woke once from a fitful dream and saw the pale moon eyes of the old man staring from the darkness. When he next awoke it was daylight. He heard the sounds of the village and smelled the cooking fires, and the friendly faces of children peeping around the door frame helped him overcome most of his fear.

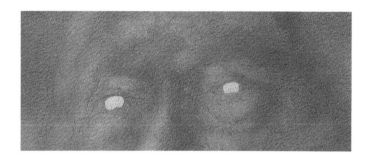

Two Moons

For two days Leif rested in the darkness of the house, periods of deep sleep interrupted by the painful memory of the attack and the long journey by canoe.

Whenever he awoke, the old man was always there, offering water and sometimes a sweet drink that smelled of flowers. Leif sensed other people quietly entering and leaving, and was happy to hear the giggles and whispers of children.

Over the next few days he was allowed to wander freely about the village, and groups of children trailed in his wake. Some of the words he had learned from his friends in Navidad were understood here, so he was able to ask simple questions and understand the answers.

The village was larger than any he had seen on the other islands, the houses more substantial, and more fields stretched toward the surrounding forest. If he could run to the forest, Leif thought, he might have a chance of escaping. But where would he go, surrounded as he was by unknown dangers to the west and the vastness of the ocean to the east?

At first all the eyes of the village were on him, but after a while only the children seemed to be interested in what he did and where he went. Once Leif pretended he was studying the various crops, and moved through the planted fields toward the trees. He waited for the warning shout, the voice telling him to go no further, but none came. He

was a dozen paces from the forest, then six, then one. Another step and he would be out of the sunlight and into the darkness of the forest. He glanced back, as though to catch the shout, but none came. He saw that even the children were busy in some little game of their own, in one of the irrigation ditches. No eyes were on him at all. No, not quite: he knew that the blind eyes of the old man were, that somehow they would follow him wherever he went. Quickly he walked back into the sunlight and joined the children in their game.

At night the old man began teaching Leif new words. He pointed in the direction of the moon and then to himself and again to the moon. Then he pointed to his two blind eyes. His name was Two Moons.

During the weeks and months that followed, Leif journeyed with the two men about the island's high forests and river valleys. One man was the eyes for the other. By now Leif had learned enough of the language to understand much of what the old men were saying.

He learned that the people of this island were Arawaks, although Two Moons was not an Arawak but a Secotan from a land far to the north, a land that stretched all the way to the sunset.

Each day Leif learned the names of new plants, birds, fish, and insects. He learned how to move "like a breeze" through the landscape, leaving no trace. The forest yielded fruits, berries, nuts, and sweet sap. He learned to spear fish, or shoot them with arrows attached to floats. He, like all the Arawak children, learned by doing what he saw.

When they reached the highest point of the island, the old man who had been their guide returned to the village, leaving Leif and Two Moons alone on the mountaintop. Leif realized he had been trained to become the new "eyes" of the old man.

Two Moons began to tell him stories. He told the story of Dawn-Light-Color-Man, who brought order to the world and taught the sacred laws. Two Moons fingered the simple cord around his neck. At its center hung a small leather star edged with blue river pearls. "Here is the morning star. Who sees the morning star sees more, further, deeper. You are the color of Dawn-Light-Color-Man. That is why they brought you to me. They say your hair shines like the morning star. I will call you Morning Star."

Later Two Moons said it was time to return. They came down from the mountain to the village. From there they set out in a canoe, paddled by twelve men, toward the land that stretched to the sunset. During daylight, Leif could not help looking east, toward where the sun rose, somehow expecting to see the sails of Columbus's new fleet. But only the sea returned his gaze.

After three days they came to a long chain of islands, which led to the mainland. Was this the land Columbus was searching for? Leif wondered. Was this the land of gold and riches?

The Land that Stretched to the Sunset

Here they were in the land of another people, the Calusa. Two Moons was well known to them, as he was to all the different tribes and nations they met as the two of them journeyed deeper and deeper into the strange land of swamp and forest. Leif looked about in wonder at the great and beautiful trees whose names he now knew: the huge ancient cypress, the evergreen oak and magnolia, the myrtle. The whole dark mantle of a million greens was spangled with wildflowers and draped with trailing ferns and tendrils. Slow black rivers meandered through these everglades, the surface of the water broken only by the buds of water lilies opening like stars in the night sky.

There were pinewoods much taller and more threatening than the pines of his childhood in La Rabida. The darkness would suddenly open out to broad sunlit savannahs with myriad wildflowers and palmettos. Wide lakes of shallow water and wild rice also provided lairs for alligators and snakes.

As they walked from village to village in this new land, Leif saw men poling canoes through these shallow lakes while women and children sat in the sterns, harvesting rice. Around the villages, harvested rice lay drying in the sun on sheets of birch bark before being pounded and trodden. Squash, pumpkins, and sunflowers grew in neat fields.

Two Moons had spent his life moving from tribe to tribe, giving wise counsel and using his powers to heal all who needed them. From northern forests to grassland and swamp, out into the scattered islands of the southern sea, his name was known. Even if tribes warred against one another, Two Moons moved freely among them, sought out and respected by all. Now, with the fair, blue-eyed Morning Star beside him, Two Moons became even more celebrated than before. Two Moons not only brought advice and healing to each tribe, he also brought seeds and tools, ideas and stories. Now more and more he taught Leif how to heal the sick, and added to his knowledge day by day. Together they journeyed through the lands of the Tekesta, Timucua, and the Muskogee, until finally they came to Two Moons' own people, the Secotan.

Leif learned not only from Two Moons but also from the people of each tribe, and especially the children. From the children he learned more of the foods of the forest that could be eaten raw; how the bark of certain trees is cut and turned back and a sweet, delicious syrup is found; he learned of the native artichoke and wild radish, hog peanut and crow potato, thorn apple and chokeberry, bunchberry, blackberry, cranberry, and grape. He was shown how to search among the roots of the bulrush for the small bulb at the turn of the root, which can be eaten raw and has a sweet taste the children loved.

The men tried to show Leif how to "be guided by the habits of the animal you seek", and from the women he learned how to cook and gather mosses, blossoms, and leaves for drinks and soups. "The berries in the shadows are not as potent as those in sunny places. Those that catch the sun contain the vigor," he learned.

But it was Two Moons who taught Leif the earth's greatest and most mysterious secrets. Two Moons described the plants to be used as charms, for good fortune, for safe journeys, to attract game or protect against snakebite. He had little bags of powders, pulverized clamshell mixed with grease for sores and ulcers, dried bumblebees and crushed alder root, juniper bark for wounds. Two Moons was blessed with a truly great memory. Experience and observations were preserved in his mind as precisely as if they had been written in a great book.

Leif realized during this time that he was being tested. There were days of hunger when he was forbidden to eat and nights of bitter cold when he was sent to wander alone in the hills.

"The Great Mystery does not want us to find things too easily," said Two Moons. "If it were easy, everyone would be a medicine-giver. To be a great warrior is a noble ambition, but to be a medicine man is nobler. The Great Mystery will reveal itself only to the most worthy. Only those who seek solitude and fasting will receive the signs."

Circle

Some five years passed, and then one day, as the leaves turned to the color of sunset, Two Moons and Leif climbed to the highest point of a hill overlooking a great natural harbor. Leif gazed down and could not help thinking that it was an anchorage Columbus would have found ideal.

It had taken a long time for them to reach the top, for Two Moons was now very old and his steps slow. He told Leif to cut some branches, set them in the ground, then bend them over to make a round top. Over this the old man tied his bison robe. He placed stones in the center of the circle, heated them, then threw water on them to create a purifying steam.

As the old man sang, Leif felt his past, his boyhood, slipping from his body.

Two Moons unwrapped his medicine bundle, and throughout the night and next day explained to Leif the secrets of its contents. There were two paws of a black bear used as bags for herbs, a pouch of otter skin containing an eagle's head and two cane whistles, a bag of black squirrel skins with the head of a cormorant and a woodpecker, four snake skins, two wooden dolls tied together, a dried eagle claw clutching a pouch of herbs and a feather, a horse chestnut and a tooth, a tiny wooden bowl and a spoon. Beside all this he placed his magical stores of ointments and charms, rattles, masks, a small drum, feather fans, and a paint pouch.

He talked of the great hoop, the circle of life and the great circular powers, the round sun and moon moving in a circle in the round sky, and the circle of seasons.

At the top of the hill they spread a circle of sage and set a flowering twig in the center and little bundles of bark and autumn leaves to the east, west, north, and south. Leif stood in the center of the circle. He stared into the darkness around and above.

The darkness reminded him suddenly of the night long, long ago, when he had stood on the deck of the *Santa Maria*, peering toward the flickering light of the New World. Then he thought he felt a movement like the gentle swell of the ocean.

He was floating, though not on an ocean, but higher, far higher. The silver ocean stretched all the way back to La Rabida. He could see the monastery in the pines and a great fleet ready to sail. He floated higher, and he could see his father as a young man, and he saw Two Moons. They were together, walking in a field of stars and water lilies.

Then Leif was down again in the center of the sage circle, and the gentle rolling of the earth stopped. Leif felt that he had truly become Morning Star.

From the north, south, east, and west, animals of the night appeared, looked at him, and disappeared. The land around became *his* world, the land of his boyhood became the dream. At dawn a great cloud of swallows swirled up, now black, now white, to where the new sun and old moon sailed at opposite ends of the sky.

Morning Star moved closer to Two Moons and realized that the old man was dead.

The Long Journey of
Morning Star

Morning Star became the medicine man, The Dreamer. The wandering trader of dreams, seeds, and stories. He grew tall and strong. His long blond hair covered his shoulders.

Two Moons was always in his thoughts. Because of the old man's teachings he could live off the land. Nature, which at first had threatened him, now sustained him.

Whenever he needed guidance he would go to a remote place, close his eyes to be as blind as Two Moons, and hopefully see as much.

He traveled to the far north, through the lands of the Montauk, the Mohegan, and the Micmac. In the land of snow and frozen lakes and rivers he gathered moss from the white pines and special herbs and heathers to add to his collection of medicines. He also collected stories from all the people he met and with whom he stayed.

To the songs and chants of Two Moons he added the remembered hymns and chants of the Spanish monastery. To the formal designs of magic and myth he added drawings of mysterious things on wheels and great ships under sail.

An End and a Beginning

After his long journey, Morning Star at last returned to the lands of the Secotan, Two Moons' tribe, where he stayed for many months. His urge to travel was stilled, at least for the moment, and he knew clearly why. He had seen She-da-a – Wild Sage – when first he had visited the Secotan with Two Moons, and she had never left his mind. Now he saw her again, and knew that she had waited for him, too. The elders of the tribe seemed to have known as well, so their wedding was soon and simple.

In the next three years Morning Star and Wild Sage had three sons. As they grew, Morning Star told them stories of his own childhood. He talked of cities far away, of the houses of stone with eyes of glass, of his friend Diego, of Diego's father the great navigator, and of his own father lost at sea. His children had trouble understanding much of what he said.

"Why would people live like that?" one of them asked. "Wouldn't they rather live here in the forests?" Morning Star smiled. "Yes," he said, "I expect they would." When the boys were old enough, Morning Star taught them to hunt and fish, and later to farm. They were strong boys, agile and bright, and he and Wild Sage were proud of them.

Morning Star was always in great demand as a medicine man and storyteller, but for years he had made only short journeys to neighboring tribes. Now, he explained to the boys, he must travel farther, for his was a gift to be shared. He traveled far and wide, but returned every few months to be with his family.

One day he returned to discover that his boys were no longer boys but men, ready for marriage themselves, and over the next four years all three married. Soon Morning Star was a grandfather, and he watched with pride as his grandsons grew as strong and tall as their fathers.

On one of his journeys he met people coming from far in the west to trade, who spoke of broad prairies running with buffaloes, of wide rivers and deserts, of high mountains peaked with snow. At times Morning Star was tempted to travel toward the sunset and see all these wonders, but he never did.

The sea still sang in his Viking blood, and he never strayed far from the coast. And each time he emerged from the forest to the refreshing breath of the shore, he looked – half in hope, half in fear – for the sails of the returning fleet.

As he returned one dawn after several days of solitary thought in the forest, Little Moon, his eldest grandson, ran up to him, took his hand, and pointed through the trees.

There was mist on the water, but the sun was burning through, and as the mist rose like a fine white curtain, Morning Star saw a fleet of ships anchored offshore. The small boats had already been lowered, and he could see the glint of pikes and muskets, the gleam of helmet and breastplate.

They are back, he thought, looking for gold. He remembered the capture of natives years ago, by a man he thought was good, a man of intelligence, and wondered if the men on those many boats approaching were good, too. And even if they were . . . Immediately he knew these ships were just the first ripple of a flood and his heart sank.

Morning Star kissed his fingers and laid them gently on the lips of Little Moon.
"Come," he said.

Returning to the village, he told the Secotan what he had seen and what he feared.

"But we have lived here forever," they said simply. "And these men may be friendly."

70

But Morning Star still clearly remembered the anguish he had once seen on the face of the father standing alone in his canoe as his family was being carried away. And so, gathering his family around him, Morning Star turned his back at last on the ocean, and began the long walk into the west.